Francine Pascal's

Meet the Stars of

SWEET VALLEY
High™

Francine Pascal's

Meet the Stars of

SWEET VALLEY High™

An authorized biography by the editors of Sweet Valley High

BANTAM BOOKS
NEW YORK · TORONTO · LONDON · SYDNEY · AUCKLAND

RL 6, age 12 and up

MEET THE STARS OF SWEET VALLEY HIGH

A Bantam Book / August 1995

Sweet Valley High®
is a registered trademark of Francine Pascal
Conceived by Francine Pascal
Produced by Daniel Weiss Associates, Inc.
33 West 17th Street
New York, NY 10011

Photos from Sweet Valley High *television series*
© *1995 Saban Entertainment, Inc., and Saban International N.V.*

ISBN: 0-553-56731-4

Published simultaneously in the United States and Canada

Bantam Books are published by Bantam Books, a division of Bantam
Doubleday Dell Publishing Group, Inc. Its trademark, consisting of the
words "Bantam Books" and the portrayal of a rooster, is Registered in
U.S. Patent and Trademark Office and in other countries. Marca
Registrada. Bantam Books, 1540 Broadway, New York, New York 10036.

PRINTED IN THE UNITED STATES OF AMERICA

OPM   0 9 8 7 6 5 4 3

Contents

Introduction

If you're a fan of the Sweet Valley High book series, you already know Jessica and Elizabeth Wakefield and all the other students at Sweet Valley High. And you probably love watching them come to life on TV every week.

But what do you know about Cynthia and Brittany Daniel, the real-life twins who play Jessica and Elizabeth on the show? What do you know about Bridget Flanery, Ryan James Bittle, and Amy Danles, the actors who play Lila Fowler, Todd Wilkins, and Enid Rollins?

We spent a few days with the cast on the set of *Sweet Valley High*, and we had a blast! They are a warm, friendly, funny group. In many ways they are like the characters they play, and in many ways they're different. So even though you may know everything about Jessica and Elizabeth and their friends, there's lots to learn about the actors who bring them to life.

Here's a look at the real people behind your favorite Sweet Valley characters—where they grew up, how they became actors, how they feel about the show and their fellow cast members, what they love, what they don't, and how they'd like to spend their future.

We'll also give you a sneak peek behind the scenes at what it's like on the set of a TV show, and at the hard work it takes to make a hit like Sweet Valley.

So get ready to meet the stars of *Sweet Valley High*. We know you'll love them as much as we do!

1
The Daniel Twins/
The Wakefield Twins

Jessica and Elizabeth Wakefield are gorgeous sixteen-year-old identical twins with long, sun-streaked blond hair, blue-green eyes, and slim, athletic builds. They share a bond of sisterhood, as close as any could be, and a love of adventure. As the stars of over three hundred books, they have captured the hearts and imaginations of millions of young readers.

Brittany and Cynthia Daniel are gorgeous eighteen-year-old twins. They too have long blond hair, blue-green eyes, and slim, athletic builds. They too love adventure and are as close as sisters could be. As the stars of over thirty TV episodes of *Sweet Valley High*, they have won the hearts of millions of young viewers.

So you can imagine that when Cynthia and Brittany Daniel were cast as Elizabeth and Jessica Wakefield, it was a match made in heaven. Although more than one hundred identical twins auditioned for the roles of Elizabeth and Jessica, Cynthia and Brittany were the obvious choice. "The minute they walked in the room, we knew we'd found our twins," says Lance H. Robbins, executive producer of *Sweet Valley High*. "They are the living embodiment of Jessica and Elizabeth. And to our delight, they happen to be very good actresses."

Cynthia and Brittany feel as though they were born to play the Wakefields. Both girls have long been readers and fans of the Sweet Valley High books, and for years have been told they look exactly like the famous Wakefield twins. Seems like fate, doesn't it?

The Daniel twins, Cynthia Lynn Daniel (also known to her close friends as Cyn or Lu Lu) and Brittany Ann Daniel (also known as Britt or Boo Boo), were born on March 17 in the college town of Gainesville, Florida.

They grew up there with their parents, C.B., the president of a bank, and Carolyn, a business owner, and their older brother, Brad. They were not the only identical twins in town. Believe it or not, there were nine sets of identical twins in their freshman class in high school!

But the Daniel twins were always special. Their beauty and ease in front of the camera made them natural models at a young age. They've appeared in *YM*, *Teen*, *Sassy*, *Seventeen*, *American Photo*, *Florida Living*, and many other publications. At the age of sixteen they were picked to represent Wrigley's gum in television commercials and print ads—the company's youngest Doublemint Twins ever!

Like Elizabeth and Jessica Wakefield, Cynthia and Brittany may look exactly alike on the outside, but on the inside they are quite different. They have unique personalities and their own ways of expressing themselves and looking at the world.

Rather than trying to tell you about both of them at once, we want to give each girl an opportunity to tell you a little about herself.

Cynthia Daniel/
Elizabeth Wakefield

Elizabeth Wakefield is often referred to as the "good twin." She's caring, sensitive, loyal, responsible, studious, and sweet—certainly the more innocent of the Wakefield twins. Born four minutes earlier than Jessica, Elizabeth has always taken life a little more seriously.

Cynthia Daniel, on the other hand, admits to being "a little wilder in high school" than her twin sister, Brittany. She, not Brittany, was the cheerleader and the risk-taker. She, not Brittany, tended to take her schoolwork a little less seriously. And Cynthia is actually the younger twin by five minutes.

So does that make Cynthia the "bad

twin"? No way. She is kind and friendly, down-to-earth and open-minded—a great sister and a great friend. Nevertheless, Jessica is probably more Cynthia's type of girl than Elizabeth. But Cynthia and Brittany both enjoy the challenge of playing the opposite of their real-life roles. And Cynthia agrees that while she may actually *be* a little less innocent than her sister, she *looks* more innocent and wholesome on camera.

When we asked her how she felt about Elizabeth, Cynthia said, "I love my character. I love playing the nice and down-to-earth twin. But it might be fun to play a wilder girl every once in a while."

How does Sweet Valley High compare to Cynthia's real-life high school in Gainesville? "My high school was really laid-back," Cynthia says. "There weren't too many people out to impress each other the way Jessica and Lila are." What would she like to see happen on the show? "I'd like for the other characters to have bigger roles," she says. "I'd like for the show to deal with more serious issues, such as sexual abuse and alcoholism."

A Dream Come True

In spite of her extensive modeling experience and some big acting jobs—episodes of *The New Leave It to Beaver* and *Burke's Law*, and a small role in the feature film *The Basketball Diaries*—Cynthia's life has changed a lot since she landed a leading role in *Sweet Valley High*.

First of all, there are the long hours of shooting: often as many as fifteen hours a day, five days a week. That's a lot of work! And it's especially tough for the twins—Cynthia and Brittany are in almost every scene.

"I have major responsibility now," Cynthia tells us. "In high school, all I had to do was try to make it to school on time. Now I have to get to work early in the morning and be prepared for my scenes. There's no sleeping on the job the way I could sometimes get away with sleeping in boring classes!"

Cynthia has had to make a big adjustment in her lifestyle, too. She's gone from living at home with her parents in Florida to living on her own with her sister in an apartment outside of L.A., not far from the studio where *Sweet Valley High* is filmed.

On top of all the lines she has to memorize, Cynthia has acting classes to attend, and sessions with a personal trainer to keep her in perfect shape.

But is it all worth it? Cynthia doesn't hesitate for a second. "It's a dream come true," she says.

Life in the Fast Lane

Cynthia loves being an actress, and she loves being on the set of *Sweet Valley High*. She especially loves "the feeling of accomplishing a difficult scene and feeling your adrenaline pumping. It's the best feeling when you work on a scene for days, and then have people compliment you on your work."

The life of a celebrity takes some getting used to. Cynthia no longer finds it strange to make publicity appearances, be interviewed for national publications, or read about herself in the pages of *Teen* magazine. She's accustomed to being recognized on the street, "especially when I'm with my sister." Cynthia even finds she's getting used to signing autographs.

Do her old friends treat her differently now that she's the star of a hit TV show? "No," she says. "Actually, they think it's funny to see me on TV. They haven't seen much of my work before, so they just sit back and laugh at some of the things I might wear or say, because they know how different I am from my character."

From the sound of it, the new friends Cynthia's made on the set of *Sweet Valley High* have been a great addition to her life. "I love everyone on the show," she tells us. "I think we keep one another going through the long hours." Believe it or not, Elizabeth Wakefield's best friend on the show, Enid Rollins, is played by Amy Danles, who happens to be Cynthia's best friend in real life. "I'm especially close with Enid on the show and with Amy in real life," Cynthia says. "She's my best friend here in L.A. I love her to death." In fact, Cynthia and Amy both love to dance, and are getting ready to start tap dancing classes together.

There may be close friendships on the set, but Cynthia tells us there are no cliques. "It's really cool because there's not just one little clique on our show. We all hang out and go to parties together." Sounds like fun, doesn't it?

"We all spent the night together the night before the show started," Cynthia remembers. "We got up to watch the sunrise the next morning, eating English muffins and drinking coffee and singing the theme song for *Sweet Valley High*."

Cyn at a Glance

What are Cynthia's favorite things? Keep reading and find out.

Favorite movie:
"I don't really have one, but all of us girls on the show sit around singing songs from *Grease*."

Favorite TV shows (besides SVH!):
My So-Called Life, Party of Five, Seinfeld

Favorite books:
The Sweet Valley High series, of course!

Favorite actress:
Meg Ryan

Favorite food:
Pasta!

Favorite band:
Sheryl Crow

Favorite colors:
Black, gray, and *green!*

Favorite hobbies:
Working out, Rollerblading,
and going to the beach

Favorite way to relax:
Hanging out with a good friend at
the beach and talking for hours

Favorite thing to do on a Saturday night:
Eating dinner and falling asleep on
the couch in front of the TV

Favorite sports:
"I was a cheerleader in high school,
but I like watching football and soccer."

Favorite team:
University of Florida Gators!

Favorite beach:
St. Augustine Beach in Florida

Favorite vacation:
Two weeks in Hawaii

Favorite place to live:
Right here in California

Hopes and Dreams

Though Elizabeth Wakefield is never far
from Todd Wilkins, her longtime steady boyfriend, Cynthia lives a more independent life.
She doesn't have a boyfriend at the moment,
and says that although she's been "in lust,"
she's never really been in love.

Nevertheless, she strikes us as a true-blue

romantic. She's sure she wants to get married about ten years from now. And when we asked who in the world, living or dead, she would most like to spend an hour with, she responded, "The person I'm destined to fall in love with."

Like her character, Elizabeth, Cynthia is totally clear-sighted and focused about her future. Her goals: "To star in feature films, and to have a loving husband and maybe a baby girl."

Her goal for the present is just as certain: to work hard and "do the best I possibly can."

Cynthia may not be just like Elizabeth, but she sure sounds like her sometimes!

Brittany Daniel/
Jessica Wakefield

Jessica Wakefield is a force to be reckoned
with. She's scheming and seductive, dazzling
and dangerous, and she *always* gets what she
wants. Still, no matter how much trouble
Jessica stirs up, you can't help loving her.

Brittany Daniel is unforgettable in her
own right. But is she like Jessica? Definitely
not. Paradoxically, Brittany is the older and
more responsible of the Daniel twins.
Brittany's more likely to be keeping her twin
sister, Cynthia, out of trouble than the other
way around. "I'm really not much like
Jessica," Brittany says. "Actually, I'm more
like Elizabeth. I'm more into school and having a serious boyfriend."

15

Brittany is a hard worker and a serious student—a member of the National Honor Society all four years of high school—whereas Jessica considers school a time for flirting with guys, gossiping, and showing off her clothes.

But while Brittany may be miles apart from Jessica, she's got the job of playing Jessica down to a science. Watching Brittany as Jessica on TV is a thrill—you'd never guess what a thoughtful, responsible person Brittany is in real life. Brittany's skill may have something to do with how she feels about her character. "I love Jessica," Brittany says. "She's so sassy and devilish. She's so much fun to play." And Brittany has found at least a couple of links between herself and Jessica: "I feel confident in myself and what I do, and I also love to flirt!"

As much fun as Jessica's mischievous side may be, Brittany is hoping to develop her character beyond that as the series continues. "I would like to see a more sensitive side of Jessica. I love her conniving side, but she does have a sweet and sincere side I would like to see and perform more of."

The Road to Sweet Valley

Brittany, like Cynthia, has been acting and modeling for a long time. Her first professional break was on *The New Leave It to Beaver*. "Cyn and I played a green, two-headed monster," Brittany reports.

In addition to the Doublemint commercials and the other roles she and Cynthia have played together, Brittany has also had the experience of acting apart from her twin. She's even lived on her own. In 1992 she spent seven months in New York City as a regular on the TV series *Swan's Crossing*.

Brittany is grateful for the experience, but she missed home, and she definitely missed her twin! Still, she thinks her months in New York gave her and her sister time to develop their own identities. Brittany feels it caused her to grow up a little faster, and to learn the value of hard work and responsibility at an earlier age.

Brittany agrees with Cynthia that landing

the lead roles on *Sweet Valley High* was a dream come true. How did Brittany feel when she heard the news? "I was ecstatic!" she says. "Cyn and I always read the books when we were younger. All our friends told us how much we looked and acted like the Wakefield twins. We both love acting and each other. It's so much fun to be able to work together as twins on a show."

Brittany says the best thing about being an actor is "transforming into a totally different character every few months for different jobs. It's a challenge, and I love it." And the worst thing? "The worst thing is having to stay focused on your character and the scene at all times while shooting," Brittany replies. "Some days I'll come to work upset or sidetracked, with something on my mind, but I still have to stay focused. You have to put your personal feelings aside for the scene."

While she's thrilled with her new life on *Sweet Valley High*, the job has required some big changes. "I had to move all the way across the country from my family and boyfriend, which was hard. But at least I have my sister with me."

Life and Love in L.A.

From the sound of it, Brittany is adjusting very happily to life on the West Coast. She and her sister share an apartment with a cat named Lu Lu and a bunny who hasn't yet been named. (Hmm . . . wasn't Lu Lu one of Cynthia's nicknames? Maybe they should call the bunny Boo Boo after Brittany!) They also share a bright red Ford Explorer. Brittany loves being near the beach, where she can play volleyball—a sport she played throughout high school.

Unlike Jessica Wakefield, who considers two dates with the same boy a serious relationship, Brittany spends as much time as she can with her boyfriend. Is it serious? Sure sounds like it. According to Brittany, "He's my first love."

But the vast majority of Brittany's time is spent on the set, and though it's a fun place to be, she takes her work there very seriously.

Brittany says it's hard to stay focused sometimes, especially when she's got something on her mind. But she, like her sister, really enjoys spending time with the rest of the cast and crew.

"We are all really close and get along extremely well for people who spend fifteen hours a day, five days a week together," Brittany says. "I'm sort of quiet and keep to myself while working, because I need to concentrate on what I'm there to do. On the weekends we all party together. We have girls' nights, when we rent old movies like *Sixteen Candles* and *Grease*. We all sing along to every word. It's so much fun."

In addition to her fellow actors, Brittany says she's really close to the hair and makeup people on the set, too.

Vital Stats

Here are Brittany's answers to some quick, but very vital, questions:

Favorite movies:
Crazy People, Forrest Gump

Favorite TV shows (besides SVH!):
Saturday Night Live, Melrose Place

Favorite books:
Romance novels (but not cheesy ones!)

Favorite actresses:
Meg Ryan, Jodie Foster

Favorite actors:
Tom Hanks, Michael Keaton

Favorite foods:
Italian food, veggie burgers

Favorite band:
Tori Amos

Favorite color:
Navy blue

Favorite hobbies:
Rock climbing, Rollerblading

Favorite ways to relax:
Sleeping in and going to the beach

Favorite thing to do on a Saturday night:
"I like to hang out with my close friends."

Favorite sport:
Volleyball

Favorite team:
University of Florida Gators

Favorite place to live:
Anywhere near a beach where
the water is crystal clear

Favorite beach:
Hopetown, the Bahamas

Fantasy vacation:
"Going to a small island with my boyfriend
and just relaxing on the beach for days."

Fantasy date:
"Robert Redford. We would get all dressed
up and go to a really elegant restaurant for
dinner. Then we'd change into jeans and T-
shirts and go walking and horseback riding
on the beach as the sun set. Finally we

would go to a little coffeehouse for cappuccino and talk for hours."

Thinking Big

Brittany definitely sees acting in her future. Her goal as an actor is "to do the best job I can, possibly win an Academy Award," she says. "I would love to play a really strong, independent woman in a feature film."

If she had to give up acting, she tells us she'd like to direct or produce.

Ten or twenty years from now, Brittany says, "I would like to be working in feature films and have a happy and loving family of my own." She'd like to get married in a few years and have two kids—a boy and a girl.

We asked Brittany what advice she'd give to an aspiring actor, and here's what she said: "Take acting classes and work as hard as you can until you finally get your big break. Then keep on working hard to get even better. You can do it if you set your mind to it."

Serious advice from a serious young woman. We think Brittany Daniel is going to have a very good effect on Jessica Wakefield!

2
Brock Burnett/
Bruce Patman

Bruce Patman is Sweet Valley High's bad boy. He's rich, arrogant, and loves to make trouble. His passions range from cars to girls, and from girls to cars. Not exactly a guy of the nineties, Bruce tends to be insensitive and loves to rile Jessica Wakefield by any means necessary.

Brock Burnett, who plays Bruce Patman, is nothing like his egotistical TV character. Also known as Brockster, the real-life Brock is sensitive, deep, and has a self-deprecating sense of humor that endears him to almost everyone he meets. And unlike Bruce, who believes that the world revolves around him, Brock is always aware of other people's feelings. But despite the fact that Brock doesn't have much in common with his TV alter ego, he loves playing Bruce. "Being nasty is fun," he admits.

Brock is five feet ten and a half inches tall, with wavy brown hair and intense hazel eyes. Both on and off the air, Bruce is incredibly good-looking. Although his TV character stays in shape by being a star member of the tennis team, Brock doesn't maintain his incredible physique just by hitting a ball over a net.

Brock works out four days a week and keeps a punching bag in his garage, which is great for both working up a sweat and letting off steam. And when the gym gets a little tedious, Brock has been known to pull off some pretty daring stunts. He's tried bungee jumping, about which he says, "Two hundred and fifty feet—what a rush!" Even more frightening to us mere mortals, Brock has tried his hand at skydiving! He informed us that, not surprisingly, plummeting thousands of feet from an airplane is an even bigger thrill than bungee jumping. Don't try *this* at home!

Brock drives an Eagle Talon (outfitted with a cellular phone) and lives in beautiful Burbank, California. He's got two dogs: a Lab named Marty and a pit bull–shepherd mix named Twig. Although working on *Sweet Valley High* eats up most of his time, Brock loves to take time out to play with his animals. If it's true that a girl can trust a guy who owns a dog, then Brock scores high points on the potentially-a-good-boyfriend scale.

Where He Comes From

Originally from Newburgh, Indiana, Brock is a long way from home. His mom, Elicia, is a high-school teacher, and he has both a brother and a sister. Brock's brother, Bryce, is twelve years old, and his sister, Brandi, is twenty-three. (Brock, Bryce, and Brandi—do you think there's a pattern here?)

Brock says that his hometown school, Castle High School, was similar to Sweet Valley High in some ways, but very different in others. While he feels that some of the fictional characters at Sweet Valley High could have been

27

modeled after the kids in his own school, he tells us that at Castle there were many different worlds. In other words, on TV we've gotten to know only Jessica and Elizabeth's clique. In real life, there are a million different types of students milling around. Brock also notes that in his own high school, "we never left our books on top of our lockers."

Although he's from the Midwest, Brock has experienced a lot of the United States. He studied theater at the University of Florida, as well as at Western Kentucky University. But the chance to live all over the country hasn't sold Brock on any one spot to spend the rest of his life. When we asked him where he would ideally live, he came up with this answer: "I don't know. I haven't found that place yet." So don't be surprised if you look out your window and see Brock setting up camp in your own backyard!

Brock Loves . . .

Brock's enthusiasm for life comes out in

just about everything he tells us. When we asked him to name some of his absolute favorites, here's what he said:

Favorite movies:
Short Cuts, Dangerous Liaisons

Favorite TV shows (besides SVH!):
*Friends, Seinfeld, Mad About You,
Grace Under Fire*

Favorite book:
A Road Less Traveled

Favorite actors:
Al Pacino, Gene Hackman,
John Malkovich

Favorite actresses:
Meryl Streep, Meg Ryan

Favorite food:
Veggie pizza

Favorite band:
Pearl Jam (right now)

Favorite color:
Red

Favorite hobbies:
Horseback riding, Rollerblading,
weightlifting, playing with his dogs

Favorite way to relax:
Crashing in the hammock in his backyard

Favorite sport:
Baseball (but he's bummed about the strike)

Favorite teams:
Cincinnati Reds, Dallas Cowboys

Acting: Past, Present, and Future

Past:

Although *Sweet Valley High* is Brock's first television series, he's been acting ever since he was in eighth grade. A lot of the actors we've talked to got their start in school plays, but Brock has a different story. His first performance was a role in an original play at church. The pastor was the playwright!

Brock has been hooked on acting ever since. He tells us that the best thing about the job is meeting new people—not to mention free food on the set! But the profession has its disadvantages, too. As Brock says, "trying to keep your energy level up in the seventeenth hour" is anything but easy!

Brock's first professional acting job was in an industrial film for Southern Bell. And since moving to California, Brock has won several small roles in television specials. He also appeared in the hit Warner Brothers thriller *Passenger 57*.

Present:

Right now, Brock is having a blast on *Sweet Valley High*. He was "ecstatic" when he found out he'd be playing Bruce, although the new role hasn't changed his life all that much . . . yet. He says that he hasn't been recognized by fans on the street . . . yet. We have a feeling that's going to change, so get ready to be mobbed by fans, Brock!

Discussing group dynamics, Brock says that the entire cast is very close, and they hang out off the set "all the time." So far there haven't been any fights among the *Sweet Valley High* gang, and Brock doesn't expect any in the future.

His best *Sweet Valley High* friend is Mike Perl, who plays class clown Winston Egbert. Brock also told us that Amy Danles (Enid Rollins) and Bridget Flanery (Lila Fowler) are the funniest cast members. "But I think I pull a close third," he added.

Future:

Brock hopes that upcoming episodes of *Sweet Valley High* will deal with "more real-life issues." If you ask us, we suggest some romance for gorgeous Bruce Patman—he may be obnoxious, but he deserves some tender lovin' care!

As an actor, Brock's goal is someday to star in feature films. He also tells us that he'd like to start his own production company and do some directing.

His Aching Heart

Brock tells us that he's been in love "too many times."

Still, he plans to get married and have children. "I love kids," he says.

Brock also told us that he's in love right now, although we couldn't persuade him to reveal any names. Apparently some things are private!

We did get him to admit that Meg Ryan would be his "fantasy date." When we asked him what he and Meg would do together, he answered, "The sky is the limit!"

"If I Had to Give Up Acting Tomorrow . . ."

Brock Burnett has no intention of giving up his acting career. And why should he? He's got a starring role on a hit TV series and is studying his craft with acting coach Adam Hill. But if he had to abandon his dream, there are plenty of things Brock would like to do with his life.

He told us that he would be happy to go back to school. He'd also pursue a career as either a personal trainer or a massage therapist. Talk about versatile!

Brock did have some words of advice for

aspiring actors. So without further ado, here's what popular Bruce Patman has to say: "Keep the faith. Never give up your dream, and study—not only books, but life."

3
Bridget Flanery/ Lila Fowler

When we think of Lila Fowler, Sweet Valley High's wealthiest party girl, a few choice words come to mind: *snobby*, *manipulative*, and *competitive*. Lila is also fun, a little zany, and unstoppable. As Jessica Wakefield's best friend and biggest rival, Lila Fowler is a key player in the Sweet Valley High gang.

Although Bridget Flanery, who plays Lila Fowler, shares a few of her TV character's personality traits, she's anything but snobby, manipulative, and competitive. Off the air, Bridget is friendly, funny, and a loyal friend. Bridget admits that she shares Lila's love for fashion, but that's where the similarities end.

In pointing out how different she is from Lila, Bridget says, "I'm poor, down-to-earth, and really goofy—nothing like Lila!"

While Lila drives a convertible sports car, Bridget gets around town in a Chevrolet Corsica LT. Not accustomed to room service, maids, and personal chefs, Bridget is a self-described "darn good waitress." She's also, in our opinion, a darn good caretaker. Bridget has owned and loved her cat, Munchie, for over twelve years.

At five feet five inches tall, Bridget is model thin and has the finely chiseled features that you'd expect from Sweet Valley's premier princess. A natural blonde—with the biggest blue eyes we've ever seen—Bridget had her hair dyed a gorgeous red to play Lila on *Sweet Valley High*. But becoming a redhead isn't the biggest change that Bridget's career has brought her.

The Background on Bridget

Born on March 24, Bridget Christine Flanery grew up far from the lush hills of California.

Bridget's hometown, Guthrie City, Iowa, is hardly a haven for cellular phones and would-be movie stars.

A farming town in the Midwest's bread-basket, Guthrie City is the kind of place "where everybody knows each other." And as Bridget was quick to tell us, there aren't too many beaches in Iowa. But what Guthrie City lacks in palm trees, surfing, and celebrity hot spots, it more than makes up for in loving families and good friends.

Unlike Lila, who is an only child, Bridget comes from a large family. Her mother, Judith Flanery, is a nurse. Bridget also has an older sister, Jill, and three (yes, *three*) brothers. Her brothers' names are James II, Bill, and John. Although Bridget's family is a constant source of love and support, her biggest disappointment in life is that her father and another brother aren't alive to share in her success.

A Star Is Born

Although Bridget didn't spend her early years in Hollywood Hills, she tells us that she started acting "the day I was born." Having experienced Bridget's outgoing and charismatic personality, it's easy to believe that she was destined to be a performer from day one. Bridget's first school play was *Alice in Wonderland*, in which she played the pivotal role of the caterpillar. From there Bridget went on to win her first professional role in *The Split Infinity*, a teleplay for Iowa Public Television.

After high school, Bridget went to Drake University in Des Moines, Iowa, to pursue her art and get a good education. While she was there Bridget performed in many commercial and stage productions, such as *Grease* and *The Fantasticks*. Bridget left Drake with a Bachelor of Fine Arts in theater. Naturally, her emphasis was on acting.

In 1992 Bridget left her native Iowa and moved to southern California to make her dreams come true. Since moving, Bridget has made some serious headway toward what she expects someday to be the biggest thrill of her life—winning an Academy Award. Even before she became Lila on television's hottest new show, Bridget was a working actress. She's had small roles in several movies for television, cable, and film—including NBC's *California Dreams* and *Veronica*.

But Bridget views acting as more than a list of credits beside her name. She takes her art seriously, saying that the best thing about being an actor is "getting inside the mind of a person other than myself." She thinks it's important that her audience feel something for her character, and she strives to explore deep emotional issues. In future episodes of *Sweet Valley High*, Bridget hopes that Lila will become a more complex and multilayered character. Just for the record, we think that's a great idea!

Sweet Valley Days . . . Sweet Valley Nights . . .

Being a member of Sweet Valley High's most popular group of friends isn't just about lights, camera, and action. Days on the set are long and rigorous. But according to Bridget, they're also tons of fun.

On *Sweet Valley High*, we often see the whole gang hanging out at the Moon Beach Cafe, where they steal each other's french fries and make plans for the weekend. In real life, Bridget and the rest of the gang hang out both on the set and off.

Since getting the role of Lila in the summer of 1994, Bridget has become good friends with Amy Danles, who plays Enid Rollins. As Bridget tells us, when the cameras aren't rolling she and Amy "get extremely crazy."

But Bridget has found more than friendship among her costars. She's also found romance! Lila Fowler doesn't have a TV boyfriend (at least, not yet), but the same isn't true for her real-life counterpart. . . .

Love Is in the Air

When we asked Bridget what she'd like to see happen on *Sweet Valley High*, she said she'd love it if "Lila hooked up with Todd Wilkins." Her answer didn't surprise us, because Ryan James Bittle, who plays Todd, is Bridget's latest love.

Ryan was a little shy when it came to discussing his feelings for Bridget, but she was happy to give us all the dirt. In fact, when Bridget described her fantasy date, Ryan played a starring role! She told us that to start the date, she'd make Ryan a really delicious breakfast. Then they would spend the day horseback riding on the beach—taking time out for a romantic picnic. After washing off the combination of sand and horse, Bridget would take Ryan to a great play. Once the curtain came down at the end of Act III, the couple would head for an elaborate Italian dinner (vegetarian pasta is Bridget's favorite food). To top off an already perfect day, Bridget would take Ryan for a moonlit walk. And let's not forget the best part of all—the two would share a "plethora of kisses."

So if you notice sparks flying between Lila and Todd on this season's episodes of *Sweet Valley High*, remember you heard it here first. Whoever said that business and pleasure don't mix?

Favorites!

Bridget already told us that Ryan James Bittle is her favorite guy. Here's what else she told us:

Favorite movies:
Citizen Kane, Whatever Happened to Baby Jane?, One Flew Over the Cuckoo's Nest

Favorite TV shows (besides SVH!):
Roseanne, Seinfeld, The Simpsons

Favorite book:
anything by Edith Wharton

Favorite actors:
Al Pacino, Daniel Day-Lewis

Favorite actresses:
Michelle Pfeiffer, Emma Thompson

Favorite food:
Pasta (no meat!)

Favorite bands:
Rolling Stones, Doors, Cranberries

Favorite colors:
Black, green

Favorite hobbies:
Dancing, singing, shooting pool, reading

Favorite ways to relax:
Hot baths, candles, music, herbal tea

Favorite sports:
Volleyball (to play), football (to watch)

Favorite teams:
Chicago Bulls, Chicago Cubs,
Chicago Bears

Let's Get Serious

Bridget encourages everyone to find a profession that is fulfilling and meaningful for them, and she has some specific advice for aspiring actors. She says it's important to get educated and learn about the trade on all levels. Bridget emphatically told us, "The best actors are always learning."

Bridget loves the world of Sweet Valley High, but she's also got a keen awareness of the world she lives in. As a result, Bridget's goal is to use her acting talent to make films that will benefit society in a concrete way. And if she had to give up acting tomorrow, Bridget says she would work in social services in an underdeveloped country.

In our opinion, snobby Lila Fowler could use some life lessons from Bridget Flanery. We have a hunch that Bridget might agree!

4
Ryan James Bittle/ Todd Wilkins

Todd Wilkins is Sweet Valley High's star basketball player and—more important—Elizabeth Wakefield's longtime steady boyfriend. Todd is big man on campus, Mr. Nice Guy, and stud extraordinaire, all rolled into one.

Like his TV character, Ryan James Bittle loves sports and values his friends and family. While Ryan relates to a lot of Todd's personality traits, he says, "I wouldn't deal with my girlfriend the way he does." It's true that Todd has a tendency to be a bit jealous when it comes to Elizabeth. On one *Sweet Valley High* episode, Todd even jeopardized his relationship with his best friend, Winston Egbert, because he mistakenly thought that Winston was putting the moves on Elizabeth. In real life, Ryan is confident when it comes to both friendships and romance. And he would never let one stand in the way of the other—he hopes.

While Ryan respects Todd Wilkins's desire to make it into the National Basketball Association (NBA), his real-life sports passions lie elsewhere. Ryan is a huge fan of both surfing and water polo. When we asked if he'd ever tried surfing, his response was simply, "Of course." He also told us that his fantasy vacation would include surfing in either Hawaii or Tahiti. For now, though, he's happy to catch a wave at Huntington Beach.

Ryan also loves water polo. For those of you who aren't in the know, the object of water polo is . . . Hey, what *is* the object of water polo? Well, regardless of what the sport actually involves, Ryan told us that if he had to give up acting tomorrow (not likely), he'd go to college and play—you guessed it—water polo.

Ryan is six feet one inch tall, and he

weighs 160 pounds. With thick blond hair and piercing blue eyes, Ryan is truly a sight to behold. For everyone who's seen him in pictures and on television, we have to tell you that he's even better-looking in person. And you probably thought that was impossible!

What He's Been Doing Till Now

Ryan James Bittle came into the world on March 21, 1976. He was born in southern California and has lived in La Crescenta, California, his entire life.

Ryan graduated from Crescenta Valley High (the name sounds familiar, huh?) in June of 1994, and he still lives at home with his family. His mother, Kathy, is a registered nurse, and his father, Jim, is a fire captain. Ryan has an older brother, Jeff, who is twenty-eight. His younger brother, Ronnie, is sixteen—the same age as Ryan's TV character. Ryan also has two dogs, Hobbs and Bear, as well as three fish, Weechie, Josep, and Guedo.

Although Ryan's first major acting experience

has been *Sweet Valley High*, he's been in the entertainment industry for a while. Ryan has modeled extensively, appearing in a variety of print ads for high-profile magazines and catalogues, including *Vogue* and *Teen*.

Of course, since launching his acting career, Ryan is the subject of articles in magazines such as *Teen Beat*, rather than just appearing in the ads.

Ryan's life has changed since he got the role of Todd Wilkins. "I'm still adjusting," he says.

As great as Ryan's new acting career is, his modeling days were exciting as well. For instance, on the same day as Ryan's senior prom, he was photographed by Bruce Weber, one of the world's leading fashion photographers. Ryan's day was so busy that he had to change into his tuxedo on the highway—but it was worth it!

His Favorite Stuff

We asked Ryan to list some of his favorite things for us. And we got some pretty interesting answers . . .

Favorite movie:
Pulp Fiction (this year)

Favorite TV shows (besides SVH!):
Anything on The Discovery
Channel, *Seinfeld*

Favorite book:
Moby Dick

Favorite actors:
Val Kilmer, Tommy Lee Jones

Favorite foods:
Pasta, seafood

Favorite band:
Jane's Addiction

Favorite color:
Forest green

Favorite hobbies:
Surfing, snowboarding, skateboarding,
lifting weights, and "having a gay
old time"

Favorite way to relax:
"Hang with my buds!"

Favorite sports:
Water polo, everything else

Favorite teams:
Orlando Magic, L.A. Dodgers, L.A. Kings

Life as a Leading Man

Before Ryan found out that he'd been cast in one of television's hottest new series, he was all set to head for the University of California, Santa Barbara. But he wasn't about to give up the chance of a lifetime. When we asked how he felt about getting the part of Todd Wilkins, Ryan had this to say: "I was shocked. I never thought it would happen to me. So I decided to make the best of an incredible opportunity."

Ryan admits that being an actor has changed his life in some pretty significant ways. He says the best part of his job is "impersonating, and having a great time doing it." But an actor's hours are long, and it's difficult "to have a life outside the job."

He also tells us that he's often recognized on the street. Ryan is thrilled that *Sweet Valley High* has so many fans, but he's "still adjusting" to his newfound fame. Luckily, his good friends don't treat him any differently than they did before.

Ryan's unexpected success as an actor prompts him to give this advice to those who dream of a career on the screen: "Go for it. What the heck—it may pay off!"

The Set

By all accounts, life on the set of *Sweet Valley High* is, indeed, sweet. Ryan tells us that the cast gets along great, "especially Bridget and me." Ryan considers Mike Perl, who plays his on-air best friend, Winston Egbert, and Bridget Flanery (Lila Fowler) to be his best *Sweet Valley High* friends.

When we asked Ryan what he'd like to see happen on the show, he said that he'd like to see his character and sexy Lila Fowler become a couple. Keep reading for more information on *that* subject. . . .

Ryan on Romance

Ryan wasn't quite as open about his romantic life as certain *other* cast members, but we're masters at reading between the lines. And the fact that his real-life girlfriend spilled her guts didn't hurt. Bridget Flanery, who plays wealthy, snobby, beautiful Lila Fowler, told us that she's in love . . . with none other than Ryan James Bittle!

Ryan and Bridget met on the set of *Sweet Valley High* in the summer of 1994, and we were lucky enough to be there to witness the great event. We can't say that we noticed the sparks flying right off, but then again, we're not mind readers. Maybe it was love at first sight. . . .

Even though Ryan didn't name names when we asked him whether or not he had a girlfriend, we got some pretty interesting information out of him. He was happy, for instance, to detail exactly what he and his dream girl would do on his ultimate fantasy date. In Ryan's own words, here's a date that may be in Bridget Flanery's future:

"We'd pitch a tent in the middle of the white sands of Tahiti and cook a seafood dinner. We would eat in the sand by the water, sitting at a tiny table surrounded by candles and burning incense. The next morning we'd wake up and surf a massive right reef with fifteen-mile-per-hour off-shore winds."

Wow! From the sound of that date, we're going to take a wild guess and say that at heart Ryan is a romantic surfer dude. But why guess? Maybe we should just ask Bridget. . . .

There's no doubt that Ryan takes love very seriously. He told us that he plans to get married and have children. In fact, when we asked him what he'd like to be doing in twenty years, he told us, "Still having fun . . . and hanging with my wife and kids."

Talk about Mr. Wonderful! It's not surprising that Ryan's presence on *Sweet Valley High* is breaking hearts all over America!

And, Ryan, we love every minute of it.

5
Amarilis/
Patty Gilbert

Patty Gilbert is fun, popular, and everybody's friend. Beautiful and talented, Patty is the star of the cheerleading squad, and she's one of the girls everyone wants to be. She's close to both Elizabeth and Jessica Wakefield—and sometimes she has to run interference between the feuding twins.

Amarilis, who plays Patty Gilbert, has a lot in common with her character. For starters, she's got natural beauty and more talent than she knows what to do with. Luckily for us, she's found the perfect outlet for her acting gift on *Sweet Valley High*. Amarilis is also a real-life cheerleader—at least she was. Now that she's out of high school and busy with a full-time acting career, Amarilis doesn't have a lot of time for cheering on the sidelines.

Amarilis is African-American, with long curly hair and huge brown eyes. Tall and slender, she's got the muscular body of a gymnast and the grace of a dancer. To stay in shape, she works out, swims, walks, and plays tennis. In short, she's the perfect southern California girl—except for one thing. Amarilis isn't from southern California.

You might be surprised to know that Amarilis is originally from a place that's as different from Sweet Valley as we can imagine. Her hometown is Manhattan. But though Amarilis is a native New Yorker, she and her large family (her parents plus two brothers and two sisters) moved from the Big Apple to Los Angeles. Later the family took up residence in Riverside, California, where they still live.

Amarilis went to Jurupa High School, then began her formal theater training in junior college. Her current acting coach is Iris Klein.

Sweet Valley's popular twins: Brittany and Cynthia
Daniel as Jessica and Elizabeth Wakefield.

Risk-taker: Gorgeous Brock Burnett likes to bungee jump and skydive.

Bridget Flanery may *look* like a million bucks as snobby Lila Fowler, but in real life Bridget says she's "poor, down-to earth, and goofy!"

Although Brittany may *look* sexy, in real life she's the shy twin!

In her Florida high school, Cynthia Daniel was a cheerleader, while twin sister Britt cheered from the sidelines!

California guy Ryan James Bittle is terrific as Sweet Valley's favorite jock, Todd Wilkins.

Amarilis says that if she had to give up acting, she'd become an elementary school teacher!

Harley Rodriguez would like to be a little taller, but we think he's perfect the way he is!

Everyone at Sweet Valley High thinks Amy Danles
is the funniest cast member!

© Saban

Can you believe Michael Perl, who plays lovable
Winston Egbert, has a black belt in Tae Kwon Do?

The woman behind Sweet Valley: series creator
Francine Pascal.

The cast of Sweet Valley High spends time together on the set . . .

. . . and off!

The talented cast of Sweet Valley High.

Cynthia Daniel and Amy Danles, who play best friends Elizabeth Wakefield and Enid Rollins, are best friends off-camera, too!

Harley Rodriguez, Brock Burnett, and Mike Perl sharing a laugh between takes.

Good friends Cynthia and Ryan find it easy to play lovebirds Elizabeth and Todd.

Jessica Wakefield, dressed to kill!

Bridget, Amarilis, and Amy on the "Moon Beach Cafe" set.

© Saban

Brittany and Cynthia Daniel are on their way to stardom!

Amarilis Acts . . .

Amarilis began acting when she was young—very young! She was in her first play when she was just six years old (when most of us were honing our ABC skills!). In her acting debut she played a Munchkin in a performance of *The Wizard of Oz* at a college summer workshop—needless to say, Amarilis was *not* in college at the time.

After her role as a Munchkin, Amarilis did a little acting when she was fourteen years old. But, she says, "I stopped after three months and didn't resume acting until June of 1994."

Amarilis has many talents and interests outside of acting. So it's not surprising that she hasn't only broken into the acting side of the entertainment industry. She's been in two music videos, and she's modeled extensively. Not only has she appeared in print ads for Reebok and several cheerleading catalogues, she's also modeled fashions for various teen magazines.

Her Big Break

Sweet Valley High is Amarilis's first television acting job, and to say that she was excited to get the role of Patty Gilbert would be an understatement. Not only is she acting on television's hottest new show, she's also getting the chance to revamp her cheerleading skills—and, wow, does she look good with those pom-poms!

Being one of the stars of *Sweet Valley High* has changed Amarilis's life in lots of ways. For one thing, she's discovered that high school can be just as much fun the second time around!

When we asked Amarilis what she'd learned from playing Patty Gilbert, this is what she told us: "I know *a lot* more about my acting ability and what it's going to take to be a great actress. I've also learned a lot about the entertainment industry."

While Amarilis loves performing different roles and experiencing what other people's lives are like, she's fascinated by more than the craft itself. She told us, "I love being on the set and watching the camera crew." She's especially fond of seeing "the set being dressed." But acting isn't all fun and people-watching. Amarilis says that her least favorite thing about the profession is "the *waiting*."

Amarilis Adores . . .

Amarilis has lots of favorite things. We asked her to let us know what kind of stuff gets her psyched, and this is what she said. . . .

Favorite movies:
Amadeus, Anne of Green Gables,
Anne of Avonlea

Favorite TV shows (besides SVH!):
Melrose Place, Beverly Hills 90210, Party of Five

Favorite book:
Too Deep for Tears

Favorite actor/actress:
Who could possibly choose?

Favorite foods:
Pizza, green apples

59

Favorite band:
After 7

Favorite colors:
Dark green, purple

Favorite hobbies:
Collecting Suzzies Zoo stationery,
doing crafts, playing sports

Favorite ways to relax:
Read a book, go to the beach or the library

Favorite sports:
Gymnastics, football, cheerleading

Favorite team:
New York Jets

Amarilis at Work

Amarilis told us that her own high school was a lot different from fictional Sweet Valley High. For instance, at Jurupa High, "no one rode around in a Porsche or wore Armani suits." She and her friends had a great time, though—just like they do at Sweet Valley High.

Amarilis loves being on the set in sunny Valencia, California. She's friends with the entire Sweet Valley gang, and tells us that Amy Danles (Enid Rollins) and Bridget Flanery (Lila Fowler) are the funniest cast members. She also enjoys joking around with the electrical and lighting crews. A true people person, one of Amarilis's favorite things about being on the job is "just watching everyone work."

Amarilis told us that in future episodes of *Sweet Valley High*, she hopes that Patty Gilbert's character will be developed more fully—and have more dialogue. We hope so, too, Amarilis!

True Love

When we asked Amarilis whether or not she'd ever been in love, she gave us an emphatic yes. But she said that she didn't have a boyfriend. Of course, we pressed her for more information. And we learned something about Amarilis that most of you wouldn't guess . . . she's married!

Yes, Amarilis is happily married. And she plans to have children in nine or ten years. Sorry, guys, Amarilis is *not* up for grabs!

What She's All About

Amarilis is a devout Christian who goes to church every Sunday. She loves working with children and tells us that if she had to give up acting tomorrow, she'd become an elementary-school teacher. She considers the members of her family to be her best friends, and she says they don't treat her differently now that she's a successful actress. "They're just proud of me," she told us.

Although Amarilis knows that her family supports her work and feels good about her success, Amarilis admits that it's difficult to spend so much time away from them. Working on *Sweet Valley High* involves long days—up to seventeen hours sometimes! As a result, Amarilis told us, her biggest disappointment is not being able to spend a lot of time with her younger brothers and sisters while they're growing up.

While most people's fantasy vacations would involve traveling around the world, Amarilis has her sights set on the good old United States of America. Her dream is to travel the eastern seaboard, exploring states such as Delaware, Massachusetts, Virginia, and South Carolina. On her journey, she would visit old "American history settings" and learn as much as she could. No wonder she wants to be a teacher!

If she could live anywhere in the world, Amarilis would set up house in the mountains of Yosemite National Park in California, or maybe "out on an island." Obviously, she's a nature lover!

As an actor, Amarilis hopes to do feature films. She'd also like to do voices for animated features and give directing a try.

When we asked her what advice she'd give to others who are trying to break into show business, she said this: "Hang in there!"

Well, Amarilis did hang in there. And if her career is any indication, the advice works!

6
Harley Rodriguez/ Manny Lopez

Manny Lopez is the voice of reason in the fast crowd at Sweet Valley High. He's a serious student and a great athlete—a track star with a heart of gold. Humble and mild-mannered, he's also the loyal and level-headed sidekick to egomaniac Bruce Patman.

While Harley Rodriguez may not be so eager to bail his friends out of sticky situations, in most ways he and Manny are a perfect fit. As Harley himself put in, "Manny and I are both looking out for our friends. The difference is, I never got in trouble as much as Manny does."

Harley is five feet six inches tall, with

black hair and gorgeous hazel eyes. We think he's perfect, though he says he wishes he were taller. (We told you he was humble.)

Manny Lopez has the distinction of being the only significant character on *Sweet Valley High* who doesn't appear in the books. But as played by Harley, Manny makes such a great addition to the gang, we sure wish he did.

Where It All Started

Harley was born in Downey, California, on April 22, and he grew up there with his dad, Jairo, his mom, Leyla, his brother, Fabian, and his sister, Julienne. His first acting experience came in seventh grade, when he played the rude schoolboy in *The Legend of Sleepy Hollow*.

He went to Warren High School in Downey, received his GED from Cypress College, and attended Cal State at Fullerton. He's also studied music, voice, and acting. He not only sings, but plays the piano, guitar, trumpet, and saxophone. The man's got talent!

Before landing his role on *Sweet Valley High*, Harley performed in commercials for Coca-Cola and Starburst, and modeled for the Kaiser Permanente Corporation.

Life Is Sweet

Harley now lives in Hollywood, California, with a cockatiel named Tweety and a Pomeranian dog named Trixie. He drives a black 1994 Jeep Wrangler, and spends his spare time surfing, playing pool, and hanging out at the beach. Unfortunately, ever since he joined the cast of *Sweet Valley High*, he's had *very* little spare time.

But Harley's not complaining. In spite of the long hours on the set, he loves being an actor, and he's thrilled to be part of *Sweet Valley High*. He tells us the best thing about being an actor is "learning and discovering what it takes to put together a movie or TV show—seeing the whole process from behind the scenes." His greatest thrill was watching himself on TV for the first time.

When we asked him to compare Sweet Valley to his high school, he told us, "Everything in the classroom was the same. Activities were the same. My school had open-air hallways, smaller lockers, and older teachers." What would he like to see on the show? "Even more real-life issues," he says.

Harley agrees with his fellow cast members that the atmosphere on the set is great. "Everyone gets along. I haven't seen a fight yet." Pretty incredible, huh? He also confirms that cast members spend time together after work, going out to dinner and to the movies.

He is equally close to everyone on the set, but tells us he thinks that Amy Danles is the funniest cast member when the cameras aren't rolling.

Quick Takes

How much do you have in common with Harley? Here's a fast way to find out. . . .

Favorite movie:
Old Yeller

Favorite TV shows (besides SVH!):
Family Ties, Ellen

Favorite book:
The Bible

Favorite actor:
Antonio Banderas

Favorite actress:
Winona Ryder

Favorite food:
Any Thai dish

Favorite band:
Don't have one

Favorite color:
Black

Favorite hobbies:
Scuba diving, body boarding

Favorite way to relax:
Having a great long conversation with a
friend over a delicious dinner

Favorite thing to do on a Saturday night:
Going out dancing

Favorite sport:
Water polo

Favorite teams:
New York Knicks, Dallas Cowboys

Favorite beach:
Dana Point

Dreams and Fantasies

An adventurer at heart, Harley fantasizes
about a vacation spent exploring the Amazon
rain forest. His idea of the perfect place to
live is on a beautiful beach with a breathtak-
ing view. Who is his fantasy date? "Nikki
Taylor," he tells us. "I'd buy five-inch plat-
forms for myself in order to give her a kiss."

A modest guy with a sense of humor—what more could a girl want?

Unfortunately, Harley's real-life romantic situation sounds as if it's fallen short of his fantasies. When we asked him what his biggest disappointment in life was, he said, "When a good friend stole my girlfriend. We're not friends anymore, and I trust very few people now." He tells us he doesn't have a girlfriend at the moment, and hasn't ever truly been in love. Don't worry, Harley, you've got lots of time!

In ten years Harley would like to be married and have two or three kids. His career ambition is to direct and star in motion pictures and to give others a strong and positive message through his work.

What if he had to give up acting tomorrow? "I'd go back to college, get a Ph.D. in radiology, and start my own practice," he says.

But acting is unquestionably his first and greatest love. Harley, like his character, Manny, is a guy who takes things seriously and offers serious advice for aspiring actors: "Always continue studying and learning about the craft of acting. Build yourself and your character on those foundations."

What a guy! Now if only we could figure out a way to get him into the Sweet Valley High books, too!

7
Amy Danles/ Enid Rollins

Enid Alexandra Rollins is smart, funny, a little shy around guys, and probably most well known as Elizabeth Wakefield's best friend. Jessica Wakefield, however, calls her E-nerd behind her back.

In real life, Amy Danles, who plays Enid on *Sweet Valley High*, is very much her own woman. She is petite, with long, thick light brown hair, hazel eyes, a killer smile, and enough energy for three people. Nobody would accuse her of being a nerd.

Like Enid, Amy is intelligent, caring, and loyal. She loves people and tells us, "I would do anything for my friends."

But unlike conservative Enid, Amy is a

risk-taker and an adventure-seeker. She loves horseback riding, Rollerblading, and dancing. She's tried parasailing and is eager to try surfing and skydiving. When we asked her what her fantasy vacation would be, she told us she wants to tour the world. (Though she also admitted that she hates to fly.) Also unlike Enid, Amy tells us, "I would never put up with the way Jessica treats Enid."

Amy Michele Danles was born on May 24 in Grand Rapids, Michigan, where she grew up with her father, Glen, a salesman, her mom, Cheri, a teacher, and her older brother, Glen.

After a year of college she moved to New York City to pursue an acting career, and she now lives in Hollywood Hills, California, with a mastiff puppy, named Princess Rosemary's Grace, and two other dogs, named Sugar and Carrie. Needless to say, she's a serious animal lover.

An Actor From the Start

Amy caught the acting bug at a very early age. She performed in her first play at the age of four. "I played the gum-chewing girl in *Charlie and the Chocolate Factory*," she tells us. It may have been a modest part, but she reports that it was the biggest thrill of her life. Years after, she appeared in stage productions of *Annie* and *West Side Story* at her high school in Grand Rapids.

Amy had her first professional acting break at the age of twelve, when she appeared in a TV commercial for a grocery store. She has since appeared in lots of other commercials, including ones for Pepsi and Finesse. She's also won small parts in three movies, *The Touch*, *Home Alina*, and *Fellowship*.

She still takes acting classes, and tells us she loves being an actor because it gives her the power to make people feel things.

But acting isn't always easy and fun. According to Amy, the worst thing about it is all the auditioning, and "not knowing if you'll have a job after you finish one." Some of her biggest disappointments in life have been auditioning for jobs and learning she didn't get them.

So it's not hard to understand why Amy

was thrilled when she landed the part of Enid on *Sweet Valley High*. She says she grew very attached to Enid during the audition process. And since then her life has switched into high gear.

Life on the Set

Every morning Amy makes the trip from Hollywood Hills to the set of *Sweet Valley High* in Valencia, California, in her black Nissan Sentra (she calls the car Marlene!). Days usually start early, with hair and makeup and wardrobe, and end late. But from what Amy tells us, life on the set is pretty sweet.

Not only does she love getting to act every day, but she loves hanging out with her fellow cast members. Though she admits there is the occasional fight, she reports that "we all love each other. We see each other so much we're like brothers and sisters." Her closest friends on the set are Cynthia Daniel and Bridget Flanery.

The cast is a serious group of actors, but

they like to laugh, too. According to Amy, "We all play a lot of tricks on each other. I can get pretty silly at times." In fact, the Sweet Valley gang has so much fun, they hang out together off the set as well.

When we asked Amy whether there was any romance on the set, she told us yes, but wouldn't give any of the juicy details. She really is a loyal friend, isn't she?

If Amy's crazy about the cast members of *Sweet Valley High*, she's also crazy about the show. She tells us she'd like to see it continue to deal with important issues that can help kids who are growing up today. She believes that while Sweet Valley is a little sexier than her high school in Grand Rapids, a lot of the issues the kids face are the same.

The Lowdown on Love

While Enid may be unlucky in love, Amy certainly isn't. She tells us she has a serious boyfriend, and that her idea of an awesome Saturday night is to stay home with him, cook dinner together, and play dominos. Has she ever been in love? we asked her. "Yes," she told us, "I am now."

Her Favorite Things

We asked Amy what she liked, and here's what she said:

Favorite movies:
Rebel Without a Cause, Shadowlands, Dead Poets Society

Favorite TV show (besides SVH!):
Seinfeld

Favorite book:
The Tao of Pooh

Favorite actors:
Liam Neeson, Tom Hanks

Favorite actresses:
Jodie Foster, Jessica Tandy

Favorite food:
Pasta!

Favorite bands:
Dead Can Dance, the score of
any musical

Favorite color:
Green

Favorite hobbies:
Painting, tap dancing, Rollerblading,
listening to music

Favorite ways to relax:
Cooking, reading

Favorite sport:
Softball

Favorite team:
Dallas Cowboys

Looking Ahead

When Amy looks ahead to the next ten or
twenty years, she sees herself acting and per-
haps producing as well. Her ambition is to

star in feature films, and to "be on Broadway once in my life."

She says she definitely wants to get married and have a big family. When we asked her where she'd most like to live, she answered, "I think I could be happy anywhere I could act."

But she also believes there are many important careers in the world besides acting. If she had to give up acting tomorrow, she tells us, she'd like to teach acting and help children learn a sense of self-worth.

What advice would Amy give to an aspiring actor? "Never, never, never give up. Always believe in yourself."

Well put, Amy. We think Enid would agree.

8
Michael Perl/ Winston Egbert

Winston Egbert is Sweet Valley High's undisputed class clown. He has secret talent as a dancer and is the king of one-liners. Winston's humor and charm make him everybody's friend, although he's no winner in the romance department. In fact, Winston's enduring, unrequited love for Jessica Wakefield makes him the butt of too many jokes to count.

While Michael (Mike) Perl loves playing Winston, he says he doesn't have as much in common with his character as *Sweet Valley High* fans might think he does. For instance, Mike tells us that if he had a crush on a girl who didn't return his feelings, he would take the hint and back off. Winston Egbert isn't much of an athlete, but Michael Perl is passionate about athletics. The ultimate California boy, Mike loves to surf. To keep in shape, he bench-presses twice a week, and he says, "I run wherever I go." He's also an expert in martial arts, holding a black belt in tae kwon do.

But Mike admits that like Winston, he's a very offbeat guy. At six feet, weighing 160 pounds, Mike is tall and lanky. He's got brown hair and a huge smile that radiates good karma. When we asked Mike what his best feature is, he said, "I don't have one—at least not to *my* knowledge." But if Mike asked us, we'd tell him that his deep brown eyes are the kind any woman could fall in love with.

When Mike found out he'd won the role of Winston, he tells us, "there are no words that can describe how happy I was." In preparing for the role, it wasn't difficult for Mike to imagine what it would be like to go to high school in southern California. After all, Los Angeles is Mike's hometown, and he graduated from Beverly Hills High in June of 1994.

Before Mike found out he'd been cast on *Sweet Valley High*, he was planning to go to UCLA and major in English. He's put his plans for college on hold, but Mike says that if he had to stop acting, the first thing he'd do is enroll in school.

Michael Alan Perl was born in Los Angeles on November 2. He still lives there with his mother, Mary, and his father, Peter. Mike also has a twenty-three-year-old brother named Stephen. The fifth member of the family is Tiberius Einstein Perl—Mike's golden retriever. When asked where he would live if he had his choice of anywhere in the world, Mike said, "Right here." And why not? California's definitely been good to him.

How Mike Got Into "The Biz"

Being a Los Angeles native, Mike has grown up knowing more about show business than the average American. He's also got more talent than the average American. From an early age Mike loved acting, because "you get

a chance to be someone else—without conse-
quences."

An avid dancer and choreographer, Mike
got his starring role in eighth grade, when he
played Danny in *Grease*. His first professional
acting job was a commercial for one of
Disney World's rides, Tower of Terror.

He continued to be involved in theater
productions throughout high school—both
onstage and behind the scenes. In addition,
Mike acted as host for two local TV variety
series, *Thrills* and *L.A. Scene*. The rest, as they
say, is showbiz history.

Sweet Valley Friends

Mike didn't feel it was his place to comment
on romance on the set of *Sweet Valley High*.
But he did tell us that the whole cast has become very good friends. "We really abstain
from fighting," he said.

The whole gang spends time together off
the set as much as their schedules allow, and
Mike has become particularly close to Brock
Burnett, who plays Winston's on-air foe,

Bruce Patman. He also told us that the award for funniest cast member would be a tie between Brock and Bridget Flanery (who plays Lila Fowler).

What He Likes

Mike has strong opinions about most things, so when we asked for some of his favorites, he had no trouble coming up with answers.

Favorite movies:
The Crow, Tombstone

Favorite TV show (besides SVH!):
Seinfeld

Favorite book:
Lord of the Flies

Favorite actor:
Samuel L. Jackson

Favorite actress:
Jodie Foster

Favorite foods:
Tabouleh, hummus

Favorite band:
Nine Inch Nails

Favorite colors:
Red, black

Favorite hobbies:
Writing, reading, playing sports

Favorite ways to relax:
Spending time alone, or with friends and family

Favorite sport:
Tae kwon do

Favorite teams:
San Francisco 49ers, Los Angeles Raiders

Real-Life Romance

It's common knowledge that Winston Egbert is no Romeo. Luckily, the same isn't true for

Mike Perl. Right now, Mike says, he's too young even to think about getting married and having kids. But he's not too young to be in love.

Although Mike didn't start dating until he was almost sixteen, he's making up for lost time. His girlfriend's name is Karla Briesemeister, and Mike says that she is his one and only "fantasy date." As long as they're together, he's happy doing anything—whether it's going to a movie or a club, or just staying home. Lucky Karla!

What the Future Holds

Mike says that the biggest thrill he's ever had was realizing what he wanted to do with his life. But he knows that a career as an actor resembles a roller-coaster ride. It was a lesson he learned early when he experienced the disappointment of losing an opportunity to have the role of Leading Player in *Pippin*.

And being an actor isn't as glamorous as a lot of people think. Aside from the pressure of head shots, auditions, and getting the right agent, there's a lot of hard work involved. According to Mike, the worst part of being an actor is "long setups, and errors that result in multiple-take shots." In other words, there's more to being a TV star than expensive sunglasses, cool cars, and adoring fans. Well, the adoring fans part *is* nice.

In addition to getting great roles, Mike hopes to do some major traveling. He says he'll start by visiting Scotland's abandoned castles, and then explore all of Europe and Africa. If that's just for starters, maybe we should give Mike a copy of *Around the World in Eighty Days*. He'll need it!

Mike hopes that as an actor he'll always be able to enjoy the work he does. Still, when he looks ahead to the next ten and even twenty years, he has one wish that stands above any of his goals as an actor: Mike wants to be happily married, with lots of love in his life.

"Perls" of Wisdom

Mike is thrilled to be on *Sweet Valley High*, but he hasn't let his success change his life *too* much. Even when people recognize him on the street, it doesn't go to Mike's head. And he says that his real friends don't treat him any differently now that he's on television.

We asked Mike what advice he would give to struggling actors, and he told us this: "Don't do it—unless you love it!"

Assuming that Mike takes his own advice, we can safely deduce that he loves his job. So stay tuned for future episodes of *Sweet Valley High*—and more Michael Perl.

9
Francine Pascal: Sweet Valley High's Creator

As you probably know, the woman behind the world of Sweet Valley is Francine Pascal. Warm, funny, and definitely one of a kind, Francine has a special gift—she can make characters on a page come alive in her readers' minds.

For over a decade, her books have given millions of teenagers countless hours of pleasure. And Francine Pascal is not only the creator of the publishing phenomenon known as Sweet Valley High; she's also an executive producer of the *Sweet Valley High* TV show. So, who is Francine Pascal? Let's take a look at the woman who made it all possible. . . .

From NYC to SVH

Born on May 13 in New York City, Francine Pascal grew up thousands of miles from the California paradise where she set Sweet Valley High. Although Francine is a native Manhattanite, she moved with her parents to Jamaica, Queens (a neighborhood just outside of Manhattan), when she was five years old. In Jamaica she had trees, a yard, and lots of room to play with her friends. Her childhood home was also the basis for the setting of her first young-adult novel, *Hangin' Out With Cici* (published in 1977), one of the books on the New York Public Library's "Books for the Teen Age" list.

Fictional Sweet Valley High is the kind of place we'd all like to spend our teenage years—it's full of fun, friends, and the best parties in all of California. Though she invented the often idyllic Sweet Valley High, Francine wasn't crazy about her own high-school years. Always creative, Francine preferred writing poetry to the rote learning of her school. At the same time, she was passionate about politics and "saving the world." At New York University, Francine finally came into her own. In her own words, "It was wonderful, everything I had dreamed it would be. I was writing poetry and felt very much a part of it all."

After college, Francine married a journalist, John Pascal, who wrote for the *Herald Tribune*, the *New York Times*, and *Newsday*. Before his death in 1981, John was Francine's mentor and number-one fan, as well as her writing partner. The husband-and-wife team wrote, among other books, *The Strange Case of Patty Hearst*—and did it in less than thirty days! Obviously the duo was eating, drinking, and sleeping their work. We have a hunch that Elizabeth Wakefield's passion for writing is a character trait close to Francine's heart!

Her Family

Francine Pascal has three daughters. She has always found the lives of her children a great source for story ideas. Always on the lookout for plots that will speak to kids all over the world, Francine likes being inspired by the real thing. So far, her method is certainly working!

Writing Is in the Genes

Francine Pascal is not the only member of her family who is a successful writer. Her oldest brother, Michael Stewart, is a world-renowned playwright. Among his works are the classic Broadway theater pieces *Hello, Dolly!*, *42nd Street*, and *Bye Bye Birdie*.

In fact, when Francine originally conceived Sweet Valley High (as a TV soap opera for teenagers), she called the idea Sweet Apple High. It wasn't until Michael pointed out that Sweet Apple High was the name of the school in *Bye Bye Birdie* that she changed the name and Sweet Valley High was born.

Before Sweet Valley High

As we've already mentioned, Francine Pascal was a very successful writer before Sweet

Valley High was even a seed of an idea. Francine started her career writing nonfiction pieces for magazines such as *Ladies' Home Journal* and *Cosmopolitan*.

After her stint as a magazine writer, Francine and her husband began writing together for television. They also wrote several plays together. With Francine's brother Michael, they wrote the book for *George M!*, which became a hit on Broadway. Looking back, Francine says that writing for theater is a scary business: "You can work on a play for two years, maybe more, during which time you're not being paid a dime, knowing that a show can open and close on the same night. At least with a book, even if it gets panned, it still exists. No one marches into the bookstores and removes it from the shelves."

When Francine began writing for young adults, she was an instant success. Her first novel, *Hangin' Out With Cici*, is about Cici, a thirteen-year-old girl who (like many girls that age) is having a hard time getting along with her mother. In the book, Cici travels back in time and becomes best friends with her own mom. The novel was later made into a TV movie called *My Mother Was Never a Kid*. Obviously, Francine's experience in books *and* TV goes way back!

After her first success, Francine continued to write books for young adults, including *My First Love and Other Disasters*, *Love and Betrayal and Hold the Mayo!* and *The Hand-Me-Down Kid*. All of these books treated teenagers like the real and complex people they are. And because Francine didn't shy away from sensitive and controversial issues, some of her books were banned in many libraries. An avid opponent of book-banning, Francine is happy that in every place where her work was censored, community groups intervened on the book's behalf.

In the end, Francine Pascal's books won several awards for their honest depiction of teenage life. *My First Love and Other Disasters* was given the American Library Association's Best Book for Young Adults citation. And *The Hand-Me-Down Kid* won the Dorothy Canfield Fisher Children's Book Award from the Vermont Congress of

Parents and Teachers, the Bernard Versele Award (in Brussels), and was placed on the Publishers Weekly Literary Prize list. Obviously, these are books that every teen should read!

We're thrilled that Francine Pascal followed her heart and her artistic principles, writing books about kids *for* kids. Her work has opened the world of reading to millions of young people . . . and it will continue to do so for many years to come.

An Author's Life

Francine Pascal now divides her time between New York City and the south of France. In Manhattan, Francine has a beautiful apartment in the theater district. Lining the walls of one room are the framed covers of every Sweet Valley book that's been published. With hundreds of books already in print, you can imagine how rapidly she's running out of wall space!

When Francine isn't in New York, she lives in a villa in France. Her beautiful home is a perfect place to write, and she has a fax machine, which helps her keep in close contact with her New York agent and publisher. In answer to your next question, yes, Francine speaks French.

No matter where she is, Francine loves to receive fan mail. She pays close attention to what her readers (you!) love best about her books, and she tries to respond to what they find most satisfying. Francine is especially happy when young readers tell her that she's contributed to their love for reading: "I've gotten many, many letters from kids who say that they had never been readers before the Sweet Valley series. If my books have hooked them on reading, that's important. It means they'll go on and read other things and become readers for the rest of their lives."

Her Work

Besides writing for children and young adults, Francine writes books for adults. Her latest novel, *If Wishes Were Horses*, can be found in bookstores all over the country. Right now Francine is working with Richard Wenk on a new series for children called "Sam O'Malley and the See-Through Kids."

On top of all that, Francine just finished another adult novel. Talk about busy! But she's never too busy for Sweet Valley! The five Sweet Valley series—Sweet Valley Kids, Sweet Valley Twins, The Unicorn Club, Sweet Valley High, and Sweet Valley University—are going strong! Since so many Sweet Valley books are published each month, it would be impossible for Francine to write each one. She would have to write twenty-four hours a day, eight days a week, to produce so many pages!

Still, Francine finds time to develop every single Sweet Valley story. After coming up with an idea, Francine works with editors and carefully selected writers to achieve an end result that meets her high standards. In other words, she's not willing to sacrifice quality for quantity. If there's anything going on in the world of Sweet Valley, you can bet that Francine Pascal knows about it!

Since Sweet Valley High has become a TV show, Francine is even busier than she's been in the past. A perfectionist, Francine reads every TV script before it's produced, and she makes a point of visiting the *Sweet Valley High* set in Valencia, California. As an executive producer, Francine played a key role in getting the show on the air. She's spent a lot of time with the real-life twins, Cynthia and Brittany Daniel, and she knows the rest of the cast as well.

Words to Live By

Francine Pascal is adamant about encouraging all kids to read and write as much as possible. And when asked for advice to aspiring authors, Francine knew exactly what she wanted to say: "One word, repeated three times: *write, write, write*. It's the only way to learn your craft. If you've got talent but are undisciplined, you may as well not have talent."

Indeed, Francine follows her own advice. She's never out of ideas, and when she's working on a novel she's extremely disciplined. While the first draft is in progress, she writes exactly four pages a day, trying to make every page perfect. Then she copy-edits and revises, continually striving to make each book the very best it can be. Obviously, Francine Pascal has discovered a recipe for success—and readers everywhere are glad she did!

10
The World of Sweet Valley: A Bookstore Phenomenon!

Today, Sweet Valley High books are something of an institution. The idea of browsing the children's and young-adult sections of a bookstore and *not* finding Sweet Valley novels is unthinkable. With over a hundred million copies in print, the Sweet Valley series have revolutionized the young-adult market.

But Francine Pascal didn't always see Sweet Valley High as a series of books. Originally, she wanted to create a TV soap opera for teenagers. Francine felt that kids would enjoy watching continuing stories about people their own age—people who experienced the same highs and lows that the real-life teenagers were going through.

When she didn't find the support she was looking for in the television industry, Francine decided to apply the same idea to books. From there, she developed a main cast of characters, as well as the fictional town of Sweet Valley.

In order to begin writing the series, Francine developed a Sweet Valley "bible," which gave a history of the characters and the town. Creating an entire world (some might say a universe) is a lot of work. Though she was definitely the mastermind of Sweet Valley, Francine Pascal worked with others to create what we ultimately came to know as Sweet Valley High.

Rather than create her book series directly with a publishing house, Francine decided to go into business with a book packager, Daniel Weiss. A book packager puts a book together—designing the cover and editing the novel—then sends the almost-finished product to a publishing house. The publishing house prints, distributes, and markets the book.

Once they'd committed to doing the series together, Francine worked with her literary agent, Amy Berkower, and Daniel Weiss to lay the groundwork for what has become one of the most successful endeavors in publishing history.

In 1984, just one week after Bantam Books (Francine's publisher) launched *Double Love*, the first book in the Sweet Valley High series, it climbed to number one on the *Publishers Weekly*, B. Dalton Bookseller, and Waldenbooks young-adult bestseller lists. Since then, Sweet Valley High books have dominated the young-adult market.

Francine Pascal's impact on the marketplace was so great that a Sweet Valley High Super Edition, *Perfect Summer*, became the first young-adult title ever to appear on the *New York Times* paperback fiction bestseller list. We're talking megasuccess here!

In Sweet Valley High, Jessica and Elizabeth Wakefield are sixteen-year-old juniors in high school. Although the twins look exactly alike, from their silky blond hair and ocean-blue eyes to the dimples in their cheeks and their slim five-foot-six figures, the girls are opposites when it comes to personality. On the surface, Elizabeth (called Liz or

Lizzie by her sister) is the "good twin"; Jessica (nicknamed Jess) is the "bad twin." But as we all know, the twins tend to surprise us constantly by switching their roles. Just like real-life teenagers, Jessica and Elizabeth are more complicated than you might imagine when you first meet them.

In addition to the regular books in the series, several times a year Bantam Books publishes Super Editions, such as the one that made it onto the *New York Times* bestseller list. Supers (as Francine calls them) are longer than the rest of the books in the series. Also, in Super Editions the twins often travel away from Sweet Valley, visiting places all over the world.

When she realized how much readers loved the Wakefield twins (and their friends and family), Francine Pascal decided to open their world to a wider audience of readers. In 1986, she started Sweet Valley Twins for middle-grade readers. In these books, Jessica and Elizabeth are in sixth grade at Sweet Valley Middle School. Also for middle-grade readers is the Unicorn Club series (six books a year).

For younger readers, Francine created Sweet Valley Kids in 1989. In this series, the twins are in second grade. And since 1993, readers have been able to follow Elizabeth and Jessica on their adventures at Sweet Valley University, where the twins are freshmen in college.

Francine Pascal's Sweet Valley books aren't published just in the United States. Translated into more than twenty different languages, readers all over the world have loved Jessica and Elizabeth Wakefield for over eleven years. And if the blockbuster success of the past one hundred million books is any indication, readers can expect to enjoy Sweet Valley far into the future!

11
History Class:
From Pages to the Small Screen

Sweet Valley High, like all television shows, started with an idea. In this case, it was an idea hatched by Francine Pascal way back in the early 1980s. Francine Pascal wanted to create a world for and about teenagers—a place where high-school students ran the show. This world became the beautiful, sun-kissed town of Sweet Valley, California, and, more specifically, the halls of a sprawling, Spanish-style campus called Sweet Valley High. Francine Pascal saw this world through the eyes of sixteen-year-old identical twins Jessica and Elizabeth Wakefield.

Although Francine had originally thought of Sweet Valley High as a TV soap opera for teenagers, her idea first came to life in a series of books.

Why wasn't Sweet Valley brought to television sooner? Francine says that she was courted for nine years by production companies and networks who wanted to make it a TV show, but she was never certain that the finished product would satisfy her vision.

It was Saban Entertainment that finally convinced Francine they were the ones to bring her books to life in the best possible way. Francine Pascal continues to be heavily involved in *Sweet Valley High*, working as an executive producer in conjunction with Lance H. Robbins, executive producer, and David Garber, supervising producer.

The Sweet Valley team also includes creative consultants Jonathan Prince and Josh Goldstein (best known for their work on *Blossom*), and producers Bill Dunn and Ronnie Hodar.

"We've tried to stay as close to the books as possible," says Mr. Robbins. "We want fans to be able to say, 'That's exactly what Jessica wears. That's the high school—it's the same color as in the book.'" Saban Entertainment bases most of the TV episodes on the 118 existing Sweet Valley High books.

The settings so familiar to the Sweet Valley reader—the Wakefields' sun-filled house, Jessica's and Elizabeth's rooms, the hallways and classrooms of Sweet Valley High—have been carefully constructed on a vast sound stage at the Saban studios in Valencia, California. The Dairi Burger has been reborn on TV as the art-deco-style Moon Beach Cafe. Within this same sound stage—a huge indoor space sort of like a warehouse—are also dressing rooms and production offices.

One or two days a week the cast and crew move outside to shoot beach scenes in Oxnard, Santa Monica, and Malibu. A Valencia mall is used as a backdrop for shopping scenes, and Valencia High School doubles as the exterior of Sweet Valley High itself.

Days on the set begin early with makeup, hair, and wardrobe—and they take a *long* time. Starring in a television show sounds glamorous, but it requires a lot of waiting around, a lot of patience, and a lot of hard work. The schedule is intense—the *Sweet Valley High* gang typically shoots an entire episode in only four days. And each scene often needs to be reshot several times. Add the time spent rehearsing, and the hundreds and hundreds of lines to be memorized, and you've got very long, very busy days.

Since the show's launch in September of 1994, *Sweet Valley High* has been a success and continues to climb in the ratings. It's already been renewed for a second season. In fact, *Sweet Valley High* has become the number-one-rated syndicated show for kids ages twelve to seventeen!

The show's success is partly due to Francine Pascal's great ideas and hard work. It's partly due to Cynthia and Brittany Daniel and the rest of the fantastic cast. It's partly due to Saban Entertainment and their talented group of producers and directors and writers.

But it's *mostly* due to you. The fans. So give yourselves a big round of applause and keep watching and reading. Because thanks to you, life in Sweet Valley is sweeter than ever!

12
Surprises From the Stars of *Sweet Valley High*

Most Embarrassing Moments

Just in case you thought that TV stars always look cool and act even cooler, the Sweet Valley gang wanted you to know they've had moments they'd honestly rather forget. . . .

Cynthia Daniel:
My bathing suit top popped off in front of these two guy friends of mine.

Brittany Daniel:
I was in the seventh grade. One day after school, a boy came up behind me and pulled my pants down right in front of my new boyfriend

and about twenty other people! I said to myself, "This has got to be a nightmare." Unfortunately, it wasn't.

Bridget Flanery:
My dress strap ripped in a college play during a dance scene, and my breast popped right out.

Brock Burnett:
I'd rather not talk about it.

Amarilis:
I walked into a pole in seventh grade and tried to play along like it never happened.

Ryan James Bittle:
I was pantsed (had my pants pulled down) by my friends in the middle of the cafeteria in high school.

Michael Perl:
I was forty-five minutes late for work at the *Sweet Valley High* set.

Amy Danles:
In sixth grade I played "The Entertainer"

on the piano for a talent show and totally messed up.

Harley Rodriguez:
My eighth-grade teacher lifted me up to write an answer on the blackboard because I was so short. Everyone laughed.

Nobody's Perfect

When we asked the Sweet Valley stars what they would change about themselves, they had no trouble coming up with answers. Who says TV stars are vain?

Brittany Daniel:
Physically: I would like to have lighter green eyes. Mentally: I would like to become an even more positive person. You have to look at all situations positively in some way—that's how you can make the best of anything! And that will make you a happier person. Happiness is one of my main goals in life.

Cynthia Daniel:
I would like always to feel proud of what I'm doing. I guess I'd like to have more confidence.

Ryan James Bittle:
I wish I had bigger legs.

Amy Danles:
I wish I could stop biting my nails.

Harley Rodriguez:
My height. I want to be a little taller.

Amarilis:
I'd stop cracking my knuckles.

Michael Perl:
I'd calm down and take things less seriously.

Bridget Flanery:
I would love to be more patient!

Brock Burnett:
I wish I weren't so obsessive-compulsive

about things always being in their place. I'm too much of a clean freak!

The Big Picture

We asked the *Sweet Valley High* cast, "If you could change one thing in the world, what would it be?" Here's what they said.

Brittany Daniel:
I'd end violence.

Cynthia Daniel:
Racism. I strongly believe everyone should be treated as equals.

Brock Burnett:
Homelessness. Everyone should have a home to go to.

Amarilis:
I'd want this world to be safer for children. I'd get rid of the violence so that children could walk the streets without worrying about getting kidnapped or shot.

Amy Danles:
I'd change all the anger and hatred.

Ryan James Bittle:
I'd get rid of pollution.

Bridget Flanery:
I would eliminate prejudice and bigotry against all genders, races, religions, and sexual preferences.

Michael Perl:
Everyone should just *chill*.

Harley Rodriguez:
I'd put a stop to hatred.

The Best of the Best

Here's what the *Sweet Valley High* stars like best about themselves.

Cynthia Daniel:
I'm really not sure exactly.
My smile, I guess.

Brittany Daniel:
I'm a good listener and communicator,
which helps me to have longer and stronger
relationships and friendships.

Ryan James Bittle:
My chest.

Bridget Flanery:
My ears. Maybe my eyes.

Amarilis:
My sense of humor.

Harley Rodriguez:
My eyes.

Amy Danles:
I'm very loving. I love people and
would do anything for my friends.

Brock Burnett:
My eyes, I've been told.

Michael Perl:
I don't have one. At least not to *my* knowledge.

Heroes

If you could spend an hour with anyone, living or dead, who would it be? Here's what the *Sweet Valley High* gang said.

Cynthia Daniel:
The person I'm destined to fall in love with in the future.

Brittany Daniel:
There are too many important people to choose just one.

Michael Perl:
Robert DeNiro. I'd ask him *everything*.

Bridget Flanery:
My dad and my brother.

Harley Rodriguez:
God. I'd like Him to answer a lot of my questions in life.

Ryan James Bittle:
Perry Farrel of Porno for Pyros. He's cool.

Amy Danles:
James Dean.

Amarilis:
Mozart. He was, to me, the most
talented musician.

Brock Burnett:
Lucille Ball.

Born Under a Lucky Star

Some people think astrological signs tell you
everything you'd want to know about a person.
Just in case those people are right, here are the
signs of your favorite *Sweet Valley High* stars:

Cynthia Daniel:
Pisces

Brittany Daniel:
Pisces (big surprise, huh?)

Ryan James Bittle:
Aries

Bridget Flanery:
Aries

Michael Perl:
Scorpio

Harley Rodriguez:
Taurus

Amy Danles:
Taurus

Brock Burnett:
Libra

Francine Pascal:
Taurus

13
Sweet Valley High Trivia

Here are some fast facts about the *Sweet Valley High* gang that you'd never, ever guess:

❤ *Cynthia Daniel* likes to talk in different "alien voices." (Huh?)

❤ *Brittany Daniel* has a birthmark on her left hand the size of a nickel. "When I was in kindergarten we had to learn our right from our left. I would sometimes cheat and look at my birthmark to figure out which was which."

❤ *Ryan James Bittle* wears a size-twelve shoe.

❤ *Amy Danles* sings in the shower. (Do you think the theme song from *Sweet Valley High* is one of her favorite tunes?)

❤ *Brock Burnett* loves gardening. "I have a great rose garden," he told us.

❤ *Harley Rodriguez* learned the alphabet when he was two years old.

❤ *Bridget Flanery* is the self-proclaimed "world's loudest belcher."

❤ *Michael Perl* says he really doesn't like prunes—at all.

❤ *Amarilis* loves reading in the car while someone else drives.

❤ *Cynthia* can make herself have a lazy eye. "So can Bridget," she tells us.

❤ *Brittany* confirms that she and *Cynthia* like to talk in alien voices to each other. "We've done this since we were ten years old, and our parents still can't understand what we're saying to each other." (Note to Mr. and Mrs. Daniel: "That's the idea, Mom and Dad.")

❤ *Amy* loves motorcycles.

❤ *Harley* likes collecting money from all over the world.

❤ *Ryan* "dresses funny sometimes."

❤ *Bridget* is actually a blonde. (And becoming a redhead for the show was pretty traumatic!)

❤ *Brock* is a die-hard romantic. (Now, don't you think he really *is* perfect?)

❤ *Brittany's* fantasy date is Robert Redford. (Guess she likes older men!)

❤ *Cynthia* has a birthmark next to her belly button. (If Elizabeth ever wears a bikini, maybe we'll get to see it.)

❤ *Amarilis* dances around her apartment to loud music. (We wonder how her husband likes that!)

❤ *Harley* likes to do voices and impersonations.

❤ *Amy* is a vegetarian.

❤ *Mike* is a music *freak!* "I can't go one day, or even part of one day, without music."

❤ *Brock* loves to drive fast.

❤ *Ryan* likes ketchup on almost every kind of food.

❤ *Bridget* would love to spend some time in Ireland. "It's so green and beautiful. Also, my ancestors are from Ireland."

❤ *Cynthia* does a great impersonation of Jan from the movie *Grease*, especially in the scene where Jan "does a little imitation of a cartoon beaver brushing his teeth on a TV commercial."

❤ Both *Brittany* and *Cynthia* appear in the upcoming film *The Basketball Diaries* with Hollywood heartthrob Leonardo DiCaprio.

❤ If you want *Bridget* to do something, just dare her. "It works!" she says.

❤ *Ryan* says he eats *extremely* healthfully—no fatty foods. (But he also admits that he *loves* candy.)

❤ *Amy* adores animals. All kinds.

❤ *Brock* loves shoes. "The more shoes the better," he told us.

❤ *Mike* sings whenever he's in the car alone—and sometimes when he's not alone. (He admits it's usually loud and annoying.)

❤ *Cynthia* loves earrings.

❤ *Amarilis* collects stationery and stickers.

❤ *Amy* hates flying.

❤ *Bridget* is a neatness fanatic. "It has to be clean!"

❤ *Ryan* drives a 1990 Toyota.

❤ *Cynthia* says that when she gets bored on the set, she and the rest of the girls "get really goofy. It's really fun!"

Here's a sneak preview of the terrifying Sweet Valley High Super Summer miniseries. Will the Wakefield twins ever be safe again?

Jessica balanced her stack of trays against one hip while she locked the kitchen door. Then she hurried across the room and placed her hand on the door to the storage room. She stopped suddenly, hearing something inside. She took a deep breath. It was probably the sound of the air conditioner shutting off. But when she stepped into the cluttered room, she held the door open behind her.

Jessica gazed around the storage room, clutching the round metal trays that she was gripping under her right arm. The room looked the same as ever. Metal shelving units lined the walls, holding an array of restaurant supplies and equipment. Drums of flour, crates of vegetables, and boxes of paper products were stacked in the dimly lit corners of the room. Out of the corner of her eye, she caught the movement of something large and dark. Jessica jumped, the trays clattering together under her arm. But it was only her own shadow, cast by an unshaded lightbulb.

Jessica took a deep breath, but the shadowy room suddenly seemed eerie and unsafe. Of course there was nothing to be afraid of, she told herself. But after the minutes spent alone and terrified in Scott's car the night before, she wasn't taking any chances. She wouldn't venture another step into the room without Elizabeth by her side.

She began backing out through the door when a shadow fell across her face. A man was standing only a few feet away, a dark silhouette against the hanging lightbulb.

Jessica dropped the trays with a metallic clamor as she threw her arms up in front of her face. Then she was paralyzed by the sight of the man's shadow looming up beside her.

In his hand was a knife.

"Elizabeth!" she screamed.

The knife clattered to the floor. A rough hand shoved Jessica aside, and the man ran past her into the kitchen, heading toward the dining room. A few seconds later she heard the front door slam shut.

"All right, girls," the tall, black-haired police detective said to the twins a half hour later. "I was hoping to wait until we could get hold of your father, but I can't seem to locate him. Do you want to try to pick out the man in a lineup? Or would you feel better if we waited until your father can be here with you?"

Elizabeth smiled at his concern. She turned to Jessica and saw that her sister was calmer now too, after the initial fright of seeing the man with the knife. "We're fine, Detective Cabrini," she said. "We might as well do it now and get it over with."

"Good. Here's how it works. This panel is one-way glass. You can take as long as you need to look at the suspects. But they won't be able to see you."

Elizabeth shook her head. "I'm not sure how much good this will do. He ran by me so fast, right after I heard Jessica scream. I didn't get a good look at him."

"Neither did I, tonight," Jessica admitted. "I mostly saw his shadow. But I'm sure I know who he was. There's this man who hangs out at the marina. He's been watching both of us all week."

"I've seen him too," Elizabeth confirmed. "And I'm sure Jessica's right. He was the same height and build. It had to be the same creepy guy."

The detective nodded. "All right, girls. Here come the suspects. Do you see the man here?"

"Number four," the twins said together instantly. The fourth man from the left was the scruffy, unshaven guy they'd noticed around the marina all week.

The detective seemed surprised. "Are you absolutely sure?"

"That's definitely the man who's been watching us at work," Jessica said. "I'm sure of it."

"Elizabeth?" Detective Cabrini asked.

"Yes, that's him," Elizabeth said. "And it could also be the man I saw running out of the storage room tonight."

The detective sighed, scratching his head. "No, it

couldn't be," he said. "We did pick him up near the marina, but not today. That man has been in jail since last night."

Mr. Wakefield was working late at the office on Saturday. He had to make up for all the time he'd lost during the week, worrying about the girls. Now he felt as if he were the one who'd been released from prison. He was free of the fear and anxiety of knowing Marin was out there stalking his daughters. The twins were safe. Marin was in jail.

The phone rang.

"Ned, this is Tony Cabrini at the police station," the detective began. "I'm afraid you're not going to like what I have to tell you."

A few minutes later the detective had reviewed the events of the evening. Mr. Wakefield felt a wave of panic engulfing him. "I don't understand!" he choked out. "The man you have in custody was caught with Jessica's necklace! How could it not be our guy?"

"This guy has been locked up since yesterday. So it had to be another man who almost attacked Jessica tonight."

"But Battaglia said the man in custody matched Marin's photograph."

"I can't explain that. I can tell you that your daughters said the scruffy-looking character is definitely the guy who's been watching them all week. But we finally got a positive identification on him, and he's not Marin. He's a vagrant named Pilchard, and not very bright."

"So there's no connection to Marin at all? I don't understand. The necklace—"

"Oh, there's a connection, all right. Pilchard finally talked tonight, after the girls picked him out of the lineup. Pilchard says a man hired him to keep an eye on your daughters, and that this man gave him the gold necklace as part of his payment."

"Marin! So where is he now?"

"I don't know, and I don't think Pilchard knows either. It looks like Marin set his own man up. He had him spy on the girls openly, probably figuring that Battaglia would think Pilchard was Marin."

Mr. Wakefield nodded. "And then Marin framed Pilchard by planting Jessica's missing necklace on him," he said grimly. "So what was Marin himself doing through all this?"

"Hiding in the background, pulling everyone's strings—"

"Especially mine," Mr. Wakefield said.

"And obviously Marin was the man with the knife at the restaurant tonight."

Mr. Wakefield gulped. "Where are my daughters now?"

"They're on their way home," the detective said. "I'm arranging to have your house guarded again."

"Did you tell the girls why?"

"I didn't tell them anything about it. They think

the incident at the restaurant tonight was random."

"I wish I'd been there at the police station. The twins must have been terrified."

"They're OK, Ned. They're tough kids. I tried to call you earlier, but I couldn't find you. In the end I couldn't put off the lineup any longer without explaining your involvement in this case to the girls."

"I was doing some research in our legal library," Mr. Wakefield explained. "I thought it was safe for me to work late again."

"Ned, you can't keep the truth from your daughters any longer. They have to know about Marin."

"I know. I'll tell them as soon as I get home. I'm on my way there, as soon as I make one more phone call."

Mr. Wakefield slammed down the phone. Battaglia had Marin's mug shot. But somehow, the private investigator and his hired surveillance man had been duped into identifying the wrong person as Marin. Mr. Wakefield wanted to know how. But the telephone at Jim Battaglia's house rang and rang, with no answer. Mr. Wakefield tried his office number, but the detective's answering service said he was at home. Mr. Wakefield fought down another wave of panic. Battaglia was always reachable. And he'd said he'd be home that night, watching movies.

Mr. Wakefield took a deep breath. There was probably nothing to worry about. But the private investigator's house was on his way home; it wouldn't hurt to stop by and make sure everything was all right. At least he could leave a note, asking Battaglia to call him.

Twenty minutes later Mr. Wakefield stood outside the door of Battaglia's house and raised a fist to knock. Then his mouth dropped open. The door was ajar. His scalp prickled.

"Jim?" he called, stepping inside. He raised his voice to be heard above a television set that was blaring somewhere nearby. "Is anybody home?"

Mr. Wakefield walked into the living room and stopped, shaking his head. Jim Battaglia lay on the floor, a knife handle protruding from his chest. Blood, still wet, soaked his sweatshirt and was seeping into the cream-colored carpeting beneath his body. Nearby a Bette Davis videocassette was playing on the television. Obviously he'd been killed in the last hour or two.

Mr. Wakefield noticed a slip of paper pinned to the collar of Battaglia's shirt. He leaned over to read Marin's now-familiar scrawl.

It's hard to get good help these days. Isn't it, Ned?

Don't miss Sweet Valley High Super #20, *A Stranger in the House*, and Super #21, *A Killer On Board*, coming to bookstores this summer.

SIGN UP FOR THE SWEET VALLEY HIGH® FAN CLUB!

Hey, girls! Get all the gossip on Sweet Valley High's® most popular teenagers when you join our fantastic Fan Club! As a member, you'll get all of this really cool stuff:

- Membership Card with your own personal Fan Club ID number
- A Sweet Valley High® Secret Treasure Box
- Sweet Valley High® Stationery
- Official Fan Club Pencil (for secret note writing!)
- Three Bookmarks
- A "Members Only" Door Hanger
- Two Skeins of J. & P. Coats® Embroidery Floss with flower barrette instruction leaflet
- Two editions of The Oracle newsletter
- Plus exclusive Sweet Valley High® product offers, special savings, contests, and much more!

- -

Be the first to find out what Jessica & Elizabeth Wakefield are up to by joining the Sweet Valley High® Fan Club for the one-year membership fee of only $6.25 each for U.S. residents, $8.25 for Canadian residents (U.S. currency). Includes shipping & handling.

Send a check or money order (do not send cash) made payable to "Sweet Valley High® Fan Club" along with this form to:

SWEET VALLEY HIGH® FAN CLUB, BOX 3919-B, SCHAUMBURG, IL 60168-3919

NAME _____
(Please print clearly)

ADDRESS _____

CITY _____ STATE _____ ZIP_____
(Required)

AGE _____ BIRTHDAY_____ /_____ /_____

Offer good while supplies last. Allow 6-8 weeks after check clearance for delivery. Addresses without ZIP codes cannot be honored. Offer good in USA & Canada only. Void where prohibited by law.
©1993 by Francine Pascal   LCI-1383-193